ROBLOX UNITE

100% UNOFFICIAL

2022

THIS BOOK BELONGS TO:

....

....

FIND ALL THE ANSWERS AT THE BACK OF THE BOOK.

centum

GAME ON

THERE IS NO OTHER GAMING PLATFORM LIKE ROBLOX!

Over **100 MILLION** people use Roblox.

You can play it on your own or with multiple **PLAYERS**.

Roblox is **FREE** to play, although you can access more on the platform if you buy Robux (see page 10). Always ask a grown-up before making any online purchases though.

The beta version of Roblox was originally created by **DAVID BASZUCKI** and **ERIK CASSEL** in 2004. At first it was called **DYNABLOX** but in 2005 it changed its name to **ROBLOX**, before officially launching in 2006.

You can **PLAY** Roblox on lots of different gaming platforms, from X Box One to your mobile phone, or even your Amazon Kindle. Roblox can be enjoyed on lots of devices.

Gamers **LOVE** Roblox – as not only can you find millions of games to play, but you can also create your own.

STAY SAFE ONLINE

1 Don't reveal your real name or age in your username. Stay anonymous.

2 If you see something you're not sure about or that worries you when you are playing, always tell a grown-up.

3 Always ask a grown-up before purchasing Robux.

4 You can restrict the 'social and chatting' features through the settings on the game and, for under 12s, it is strictly filtered too.

5 Always be friendly, patient, welcoming and respectful when playing. Treat other players as you would like to be treated and you will help contribute to a kind online gaming community.

READY PLAYER 1?

CAN YOU SPOT ALL THE AVATARS SHOWN IN THE PANEL IN THE GAME BELOW?

SPOT IT

CAN YOU SPOT 8 DIFFERENCES BETWEEN THE PICTURES BELOW?

AMAZING AVATAR

READ ON FOR HOW TO ENSURE YOUR ROBLOX AVATAR IS AS AWESOME AS YOU ARE!

When choosing an avatar on Roblox you can opt for a simple R6 version or a more complicated R15 version. R6 avatars are split into 6 body parts and R15s are made up of 15 parts. You can also make your avatar bigger or smaller if you opt for an R15 version.

Think carefully and creatively when making your avatar as it represents you within the gaming world. Make sure you create one to reflect your true gaming genius and unique personality.

You can customise the skin, hair, head, face, body, clothing and animation on your avatar.

Different developers create unique characters for their games, so you can only get certain 'looks' by playing those games. So the more games you explore, the more choice you'll have.

You can shop till you drop for your avatar in the Catalog. Here you'll find every clothing item and accessory imaginable to customise your avatar.

If you are feeling exhausted reading about creating your own avatar, let alone actually making one, don't worry. You can simply choose a pre-made one.

GO SHOPPING

EVERY TIME YOU PLAY ON ROBLOX YOU CAN COLLECT ITEMS OR BUY THEM WITH ROBUX.

THE CATALOG is a one-stop shop for everything you need within Roblox. From accessories and clothes to awesome tools and gear.

If you search on the **NEW** or **FEATURED** sections within the Catalog, you can jump straight to the latest and most popular items. Scroll down though to flip through pages and pages of other items, or search by a keyword, for example hats or horns, or by a specific genre, for example sci-fi, adventure or sports.

The more you play on Roblox, the more you'll collect. You'll end up with all sorts of items which you can keep track of on your **INVENTORY** page. You can view them in full or by category. Even better, you can take a sneaky peek at what other players have in their inventories and even buy items from them, with Robux.

ROBUX are the virtual currency used in Roblox. You can play for free but premium items in Roblox cost Robux, which have to be bought with real cash. They can be purchased through the game or as a gift card in a shop. Always ask a grown-up before making any online purchases though.

SHOPPING SUDOKU

DOODLE IN A PROP TO THE GRID BELOW, SO EVERY PROP APPEARS ONLY ONCE IN EVERY ROW AND COLUMN.

1

Now doodle an accessory, so there is only one of each in every row and column in this grid.

2

YOUR FAVES

SHARE YOUR GAMING PREFERENCES IN THE SPACE BELOW.

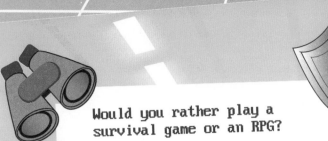

Would you rather play a survival game or an RPG?

....

If you had to face a spooky enemy would you rather it be a vampire or a zombie?

....

Would you rather be a superhero or a villain?

....

Would you rather plan a heist or stop a heist?

....

Would you rather race around a track in a go-kart or on foot?

....

If you ran a snack bar would you sell pizzas or ice cream?

....

My fave Roblox game is:

....

My least fave Roblox game is:

....

ODD AVATAR OUT

DRAW A CIRCLE AROUND THE ODD ONE OUT IN EACH ROW.

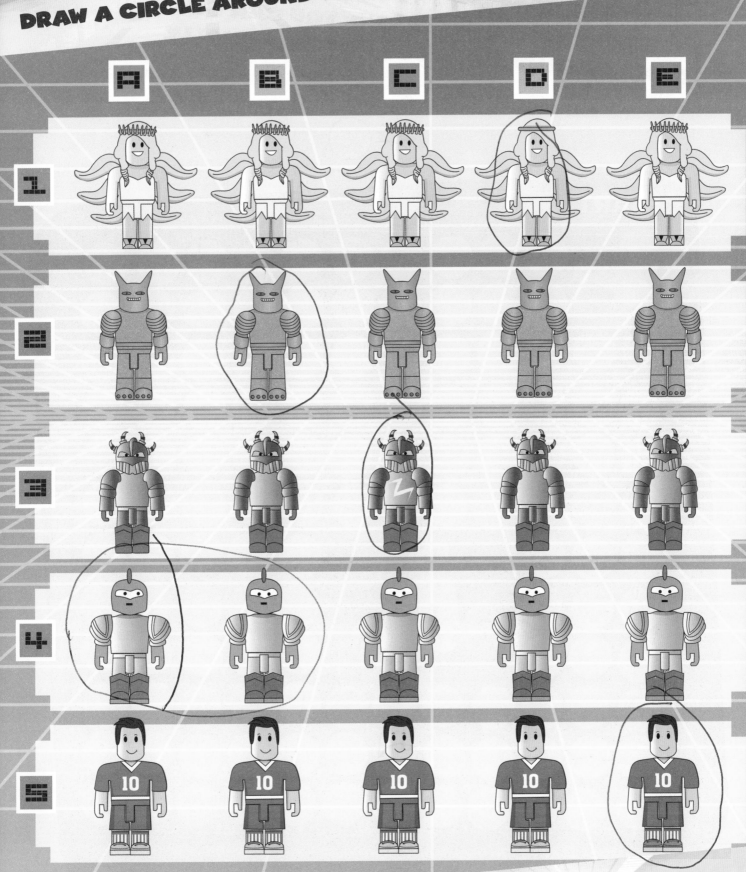

13

CREEPY CRAWLIES

FOLLOW THE SPOTS IN THE ORDER BELOW TO HELP THE SPIDER REACH HIS FRIEND. YOU CAN GO UP, DOWN, LEFT AND RIGHT BUT NOT DIAGONALLY.

START

END

NUMBER TOWERS

PLACE A NUMBER IN EVERY CIRCLE TO COMPLETE THE TOWER. THE VALUE IN EACH CIRCLE IS THE SUM OF THE NUMBERS IN THE TWO CIRCLES DIRECTLY BELOW IT.

Before you start can you guess which tower will have the highest number at the top?

A

15
13 14
10 11 12
6 7 8 9
1 2 3 4 5

B

45
29 42
36 33 36
18 21 24 27
3 6 9 12 15

C

16
1 5
1 5 10
10 1 5 10
1 5 10 1 5

D

8
7 70
50 6 60
30 4 40 5
1 10 2 20 3

MIND THE GAP

GRAB YOUR PENS, FILL IN THE GAPS OF THESE AVATAR PICS THEN ADD SOME COLOURS TO FINISH THEM OFF.

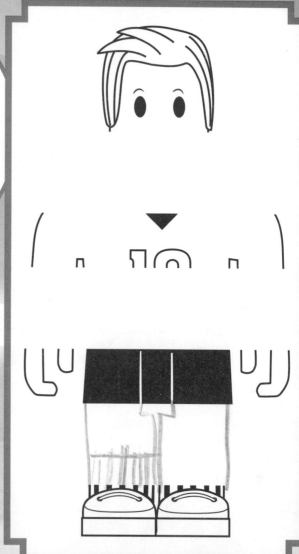

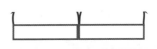

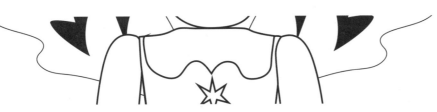

WORD IT OUT

CAN YOU SPOT ALL THESE WORDS IN THE GRID OPPOSITE?

- ☑ GAME
- ☑ PLAY
- ☑ PLAYER
- ☑ WIN
- ☑ LOSE
- ☑ SCREEN
- ☑ CREATE

- ☑ VIRTUAL
- ☑ CURRENCY
- ☐ CHALLENGE
- ☑ AVATAR
- ☑ DOWNLOAD
- ☑ MOBILE
- ☑ GUIDE
- ☑ SELL

- ☐ BUY
- ☑ BUILD
- ☑ EXPLORE
- ☑ TRADE
- ☑ REWARD
- ☑ SURVIVE
- ☑ SKILLS
- ☑ CODING

DTEEEROLPXEHXKC
USMTREWARDZLDSH
WAOVAZLSHJOSEUA
GUVRQEKZASELLRL
XPLAYIRVECUVUVL
TRELLGACWBOADIE
PNALNTPHIAKEZVN
ERSIAHFLNUIIVEG
WLDREPARNEERCSE
EOIDCULDAOLNWOD
CDIBTBZAQZFBYBE
LUARONUNYEMUNOY
GDIRXMIYGEJIXXP
JVILTFNRYLRLLJY
CURRENCYMHBDEIG

GAME MAKER

IF YOU DREAM OF CREATING GAMES, NOT JUST PLAYING THE
FOLLOW THESE SIMPLE STEPS TO CREATE A GAME PLAN.

First of all brainstorm what kind of game you might like to create. Tick one of the options below.

- ☑ OBBY
- ☐ ADVENTURE
- ☐ RPG
- ☐ SPORT/ACTIVITY
- ☐ SURVIVAL
- ☐ CITY/TOWN
- ☐ OTHER

How many players will your game have?

- ☐ SOLO
- ☑ MULTIPLAYER

What kind of world will it take place in?

- ☐ FANTASY
- ☐ SCI-FI
- ☐ SPOOKY
- ☐ REAL WORLD
- ☑ FUTURISTIC
- ☐ HISTORIC
- ☐ SPACE

What kind of surroundings will it take place in?

- ☐ COUNTRYSIDE
- ☐ CITY
- ☐ CASTLE
- ☐ UNDERWATER
- ☐ SNOWY MOUNTAINS
- ☐ DESERT
- ☐ JUNGLE
- ☐ FOREST
- ☑ VOLCANO VALLEY
- ☐ DESERT ISLAND

Write a list of games you really love and the reason why they're so much fun.

....
....
....
....
....
....

Now think of 3 fun things you want to include in your game.

1. Hoverboards
2. Teleporter
3. Guns

What is the main objective
of your game?

☐ TO SURVIVE
☐ SCORE POINTS
☑ MAKE MONEY
☐ MAKE SOMETHING
☐ ROLE PLAY A LIFE
☐ SAVE A LIFE

What kind of avatars will
you include in your game?

☐ HUMAN
☐ ANIMAL
☐ HISTORIC FIGURE
☐ SPACE ALIEN
☐ MONSTER
☑ SUPERHERO

What kind of obstacles will
players encounter?

☐ EXTREME WEATHER
☐ MONSTER ATTACKS
☐ FINDING FOOD
☑ GETTING LOST
☑ OTHER PLAYER ATTACKS

What vehicles will your
players be able to access?

☑ PLANE
☐ BOAT
☑ HELICOPTER
☑ MOPED
☐ CAR

Which accessories will you
include?

☑ AXE
☐ HAMMER
☐ BACKPACK
☐ MAP
☐ BINOCULARS
☐ SHOPPING TROLLEY
☐ MUSICAL INSTRUMENT
☐ SKATEBOARD
☐ SURFBOARD

Use the space below to draw a screenshot of your game.

Write a name for your game here:

Obby

21

COLOUR CODING
FOLLOW THE COLOUR KEY TO TRANSFORM THESE AVATARS WITH YOUR BRIGHTEST COLOURS.

COLOUR KEY
1 = ORANGE
2 = BLUE
3 = RED
4 = GREEN
5 = YELLOW
6 = BROWN
7 = PURPLE
8 = PALE BLUE
9 = PINK

23

SPOT THE DIFFERENCE

THE SMALL PICS MAY LOOK THE SAME AS THE BIG ONE BUT THERE IS SOMETHING DIFFERENT IN EACH ONE. CAN YOU SPOT WHAT?

A

B

C

D

MATCH UP

CAN YOU MATCH THESE ITEMS INTO PAIRS?

MUNCH BUNCH

WHICH OF THESE HUNGRY WORKERS WILL MAKE IT THROUGH THE MAZE TO REACH THE PIZZA?

CODE CRACKING

HOW QUICKLY CAN YOU COMPLETE THE PUZZLES BELOW?

1 Can you make 10 new words out of the letters below?

ROBLOX
UNITE

BOX
NO
....
....
....
....
....
....
....
....

2 Change every letter to the next letter of the alphabet to reveal what this avatar needs to get to the next level.

ONHMSR

P O I N T S

3 Circle every other letter to reveal this avatar's fave type of game.

T O Q B
K B G Y

Obby

4 Cross out every letter that appears twice to reveal what type of game this avatar is winning.

X B R T W
Q D L P X D
B L G T Q W

....

B l

25

EAT, SLEEP, PLAY, REPEAT

WHATEVER KIND OF GAME YOU LIKE TO PLAY, ROBLOX HAS IT COVERED WITH A HUGE VARIETY OF GENRES TO CHOOSE FROM.

STARRING ROLE!

RPG or role-playing games are a must for those who want to escape their own reality and exist in a game as someone else. Experience life as a superhero, chef, pirate or rock star – you can be anything you want to be.

CITY LIVING

TOWN/CITY games are set in a town or city – and mostly involve role playing and socialising. Sometimes you get to explore the place, sometimes help build it and usually always enjoy the kinds of things you get to do in a town or city, from shopping to hanging out at the local ice rink or pizza place.

KEEP ON MOVING!

That's the motto for **OBBY** games, which involve all kinds of crazy obstacle courses. There are loads to choose from and the aim of the game is to reach the end of the course, before you get knocked out.

HEROIC GAMER

EXPLORING and **ADVENTURE** games are perfect for heroic gamers who love a challenge. Discover new worlds, embark on a quest and complete the game to save the day.

CONTINUED....

CONTINUED....

SURVIVAL OF THE FITTEST

SURVIVAL games are similar to adventure games and can take place anywhere, in real-life or fantasy settings. They usually involve a quest or a mission and the aim of the game is to stay alive.

READY AIM FIRE!

FPS stands for first person shooters and are games in which you get to blast and blast away at other players, while trying to avoid getting blasted and shot at yourself.

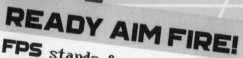

CAN YOU KICK IT?
YES YOU CAN! There are so many sporting games on Roblox, it's a mini sporting event itself in just choosing one. From football and fencing to bowling and basketball – you can try out all kinds of sports by yourself or with your friends. Game on!

WATCH OUT FOR IMPOSTERS!
Yes, some naughty Roblox creators name and design their games so they're similar to the most popular games on the platform, to fool players into checking them out. Always make sure you're playing the real deal and beware the fakes.

SUPER SEEKER

THE AVATARS ARE PLAYING HIDE AND SEEK.
TICK THEM OFF WHEN YOU SPOT THEM IN THE GAME.

OPEN

SPACE TRAVEL
WHICH OF THESE SCI FI AVATARS WILL REACH THE MOON FIRST?

A
B
C
D

SUPER SPOTTER

CAN YOU SPOT 6 DIFFERENCES BETWEEN THE PICTURES BELOW?

AVATAR SPOTTER

CAN YOU SPOT AN AVATAR IN THE GROUP BELOW THAT IS EXACTLY THE SAME AS THIS ONE?

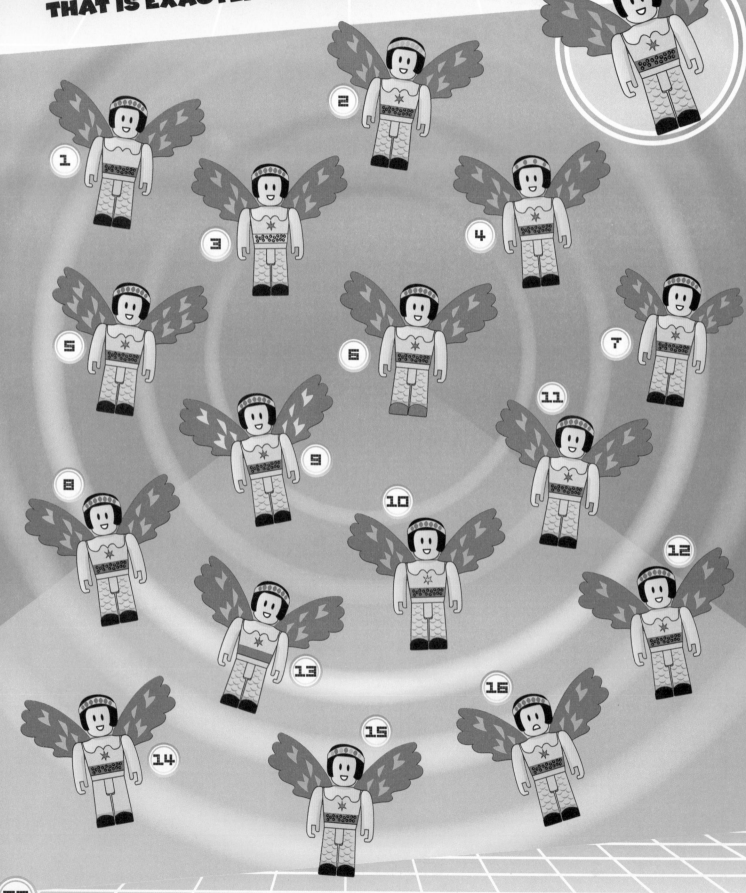

36

X MARKS THE SPOT

DANGER ALERT! THERE'S A ROBBER ON THE LOOSE. HELP THE POLICE TRACK HIM DOWN BY FOLLOWING THE CLUES, AND MARKING THE CRIMINAL'S LOCATION WITH AN X ON THE MAP.

1. Move north 6 spaces from start.

2. Go east 2 spaces.

3. Head south 3 spaces.

4. Turn west 4 spaces.

5. GOTCHA! Mark an x on the map and arrest the robber.

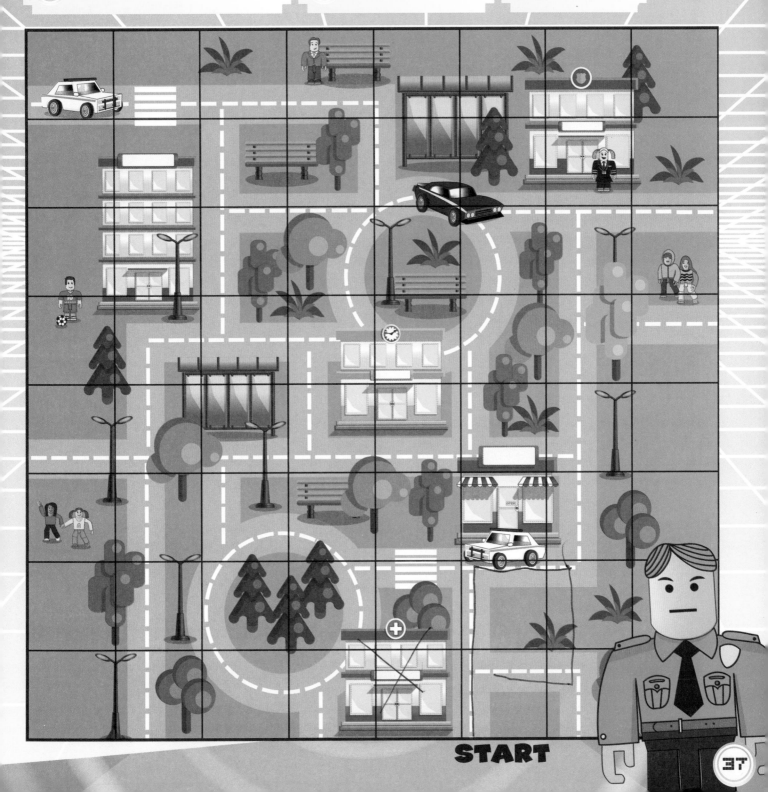

START

35

ODD ONE OUT

CAN YOU SPOT THE ODD AVATAR OUT IN EACH ROW?

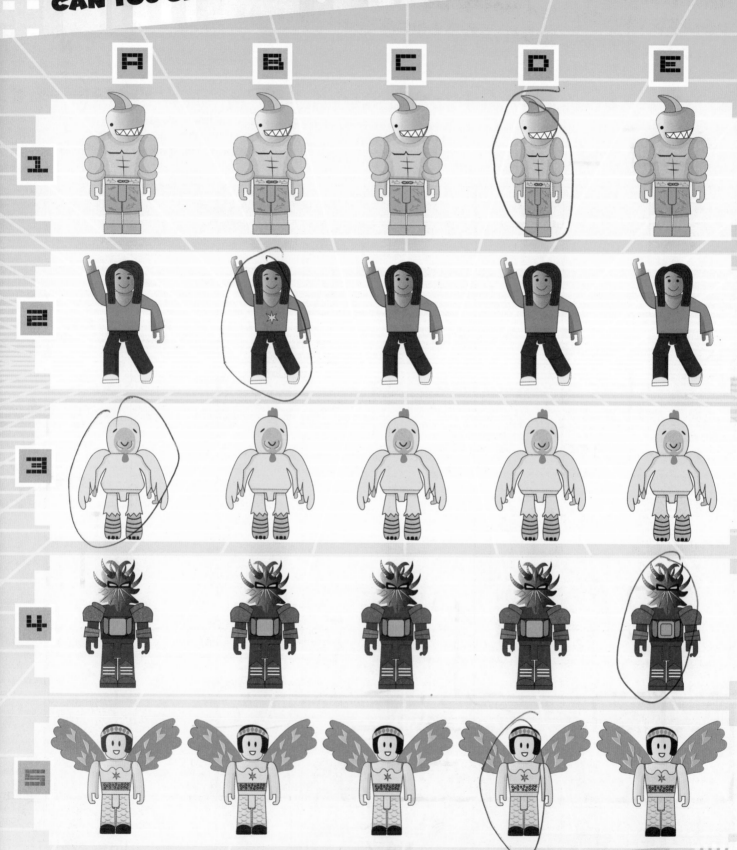

SPECIAL DELIVERY

SET A TIMER FOR 20 SECONDS AND HELP PIZZA MAN MAKE HIS DELIVERY BEFORE HE RUNS OUT OF TIME.

START

END

FAN FAVOURITES

CHECK OUT THE MOST POPULAR GAMES ON THE PLATFORM – THEN GIVE THEM YOUR OWN RATING.

NATURAL DISASTER SURVIVAL

Imagine being stuck on a desert island, with only seconds before catastrophe strikes. You don't have much time to work out how to survive... and if you do, you move on to the next disaster. You'll face blizzards, sandstorms, tornadoes... Good luck!

BEST THING ABOUT THIS GAME

....

WORST THING ABOUT THIS GAME

....

THEME PARK TYCOON 2

Create your own theme park with epic rides, awesome attractions and tasty snack stalls. You can build it alone or invite friends to work with you as a team.

BEST THING ABOUT THIS GAME

....

WORST THING ABOUT THIS GAME

....

ADOPT ME!

This super-cute game enables you to create a whole family online – you choose to be a baby or parent and enjoy lots of role-playing as you look after your family and build a home for you all to live in.

BEST THING ABOUT THIS GAME

....

WORST THING ABOUT THIS GAME

....

WORK AT A PIZZA PLACE

You'll be exhausted after playing this game as you need to manage a pizza restaurant, look after the customers, take their orders, cook the pizzas, manage the staff and above all – don't burn the place down. Guaranteed to make you hungry.

BEST THING ABOUT THIS GAME

....

WORST THING ABOUT THIS GAME

....

MEEP CITY

Up to 100 players can play this game at one time, and enjoy life in a virtual world. You can enjoy a party, race go-karts, send your friends gifts and even teleport to your favourite places within the game.

👍 ☐ 👎 ☐

BEST THING ABOUT THIS GAME

....

WORST THING ABOUT THIS GAME

....

FLEE THE FACILITY

If you're brave enough this spooky game is great fun. It's a bit like a scary game of hide and seek, where you need to escape the facility and avoid being captured by the beast (and frozen by it)!

👍 ☐ 👎 ☐

BEST THING ABOUT THIS GAME

....

WORST THING ABOUT THIS GAME

....

WELCOME TO BLOXBURG

Experience life in the virtual world of Bloxburg and enjoy role-playing, building a house, buying a vehicle, getting a job and basically pretending to be a grown-up.

👍 ☐ 👎 ☐

BEST THING ABOUT THIS GAME

....

WORST THING ABOUT THIS GAME

....

SUPER HERO TYCOON

Live the dream and build your own superhero business. Be warned though as there are other heroes out there, battling for business too.

👍 ☐ 👎 ☐

BEST THING ABOUT THIS GAME

....

WORST THING ABOUT THIS GAME

....

ROYAL HIGH

Study hard, enjoy your classes and you can graduate as a princess or prince from this magical school.

👍 ☐ 👎 ☐

BEST THING ABOUT THIS GAME

....

WORST THING ABOUT THIS GAME

....

JAILBREAK

Choose a team, either police, prisoners or criminals and work together as a team to plan a jailbreak, plot a heist or stop the robbery and catch the criminals.

👍 ☐ 👎 ☐

BEST THING ABOUT THIS GAME

....

WORST THING ABOUT THIS GAME

....

ROBLOX RULES

GRAB YOUR PENS AND GET THESE AVATARS
READY TO PLAY WITH YOUR BRIGHTEST COLOURS.

HOW MANY CAN YOU SPOT?

43

GAMING TIPS

CHECK OUT THESE TOP TIPS TO GET THE MOST OUT OF YOUR ONLINE GAME TIME.

COOL CODES

You have to pay for Robux but some game creators often hide codes within their games that give away free things – so keep an eye out for them when you're playing.

TEAM PLAYER

Playing on your own is fun, but playing with your mates is even better. Find your friends online and you can play together. You can also chat and find their games to play too. Teamwork makes the dreamwork!

THUMBS UP

Giving a thumbs up to a game will show your friends that you like it and help others decide whether to play it or not too.

ALL YOUR FAVES

Mark all the games you love with a star and they'll be added to your favourites list – making it easy to find them next time you play.

TOP CHOICE

When looking for new games try searching under Top Rated – as this will bring up all the games that other players like best.

KINDNESS IS KING

Treat other players how you want to be treated and you'll help keep the Roblox community a happy one. If you don't, you might end up being reported and banned from playing.

ALWAYS ASK A GROWN-UP BEFORE GOING ONLINE.

ROBLOX GENIUS

POWER UP YOUR BRAIN AND YOUR GAMING SKILLS WITH SOME GREAT ONLINE ROBLOX TOOLS.

✳ Roblox **STUDIO** enables you to create anything you can imagine. Whether you're a novice or an experienced programmer, you can create your own game using the tools available.

✳ From manipulation of objects or terrain, to creating complex coding scripts and game functions – Roblox Studio can help you do it all.

✳ Roblox Studio also allows you to test your games in an isolated environment before uploading them to the Roblox gaming site.

✳ If you love creating games on Roblox but want to learn new skills, check out Roblox **EDUCATION**. It offers free resources to teachers and students to develop skills in all areas of game creation, from coding to design. Anyone can build a game on Roblox – even if you've never coded before. You can find lesson plans, coding tips, tutorials and full game-creation projects.

✳ Lua is the simple programming language used in Roblox and on Roblox Education you can learn the essentials: including strings, arrays and loops.

ANSWERS

PAGES 6-7

PAGE 8

PAGE 11

PAGE 13

1-D 2-B 3-C

4-A 5-E

PAGE 14

START

END

PAGE 15

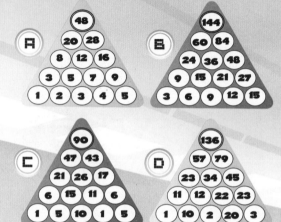

A
48
20 28
8 12 16
3 5 7 9
1 2 3 4 5

B
144
60 84
24 36 48
9 15 21 27
3 6 9 12 15

C
90
47 43
21 26 17
6 15 11 6
1 5 10 1 5

D
136
57 79
23 34 45
11 12 22 23
1 10 2 20 3

PAGES 18-19

D T E E R O L P X E H X K C
U S M T R E W A R D Z L D S H
W A O V A Z L S H J O S E U A
G U V R Q E K Z A S E L L R L
X P L A Y I R V E C U V U V L
T R E L L G A C W B O A D I E
P N A L N T P H I A K E Z V N
E R S I A H F L N U I I V E G
W L D R E P A R N E E R C S E
E O I D C U L D A O L N W O D
C D I B T B Z A Q Z F B Y B E
L U A R O N U N Y E M U N O Y
G D I R X M I Y G E J I X X P
J V I L T F N R Y L R L L J Y
C U R R E N C Y M H B D E I G

PAGE 24

A

B

C

D

PAGE 25

1-17, 2-29, 3-39, 4-11, 5-36, 6-7, 8-34,
9-27, 10-30, 12-31, 13-37, 14-40, 15-38,
16-23, 18-33, 19-26, 20-25, 21-35, 22-28,
24-32